THE VERY HUNGRY CATERPILLAR

by Eric Carle

COLLINS PUBLISHERS
NEW YORK · CLEVELAND

Published by William Collins Publishers Incorporated.
2080 West 117th Street, Cleveland, Ohio 44111

Library of Congress Cataloging in Publication Data
Carle, Eric.
The very hungry caterpillar.
SUMMARY: Follows the progress of a hungry little
caterpillar as he eats his way through a varied and very
large quantity of food until, full at last, he forms a
cocoon around himself and goes to sleep.
    [1. Caterpillars — Fiction] I. Title.
PZ7.C21476Ve   [E]   79-13202
ISBN 0-529-00775-4
ISBN 0-529-00776-2 lib. bdg.
Tenth Printing July 1979

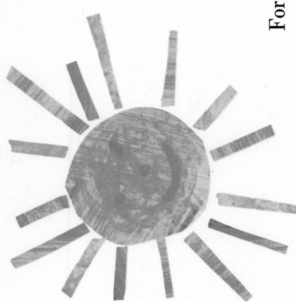

For my sister Christa

In the light of the moon
a little egg lay on a leaf.

One Sunday morning the warm sun came up and—pop!—out of the egg came a tiny and very hungry caterpillar.

He started to look for some food.

On Wednesday
he ate through
three plums,
but he was still
hungry.

On Saturday
he ate through
one piece of
chocolate cake, one ice-cream cone, one pickle, one slice of Swiss cheese, one slice of salami,

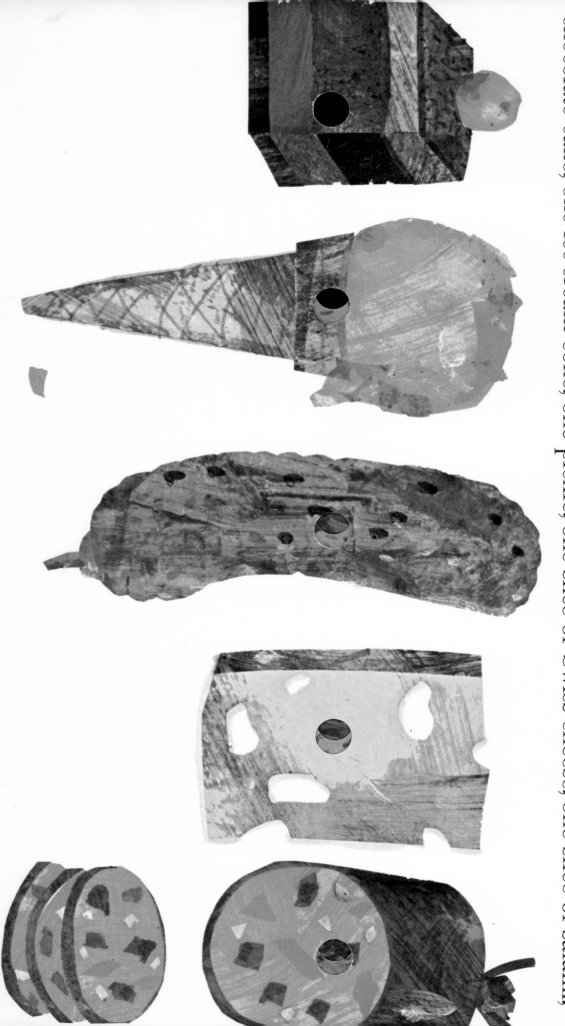

one lollipop, one piece of cherry pie, one sausage, one cupcake, and one slice of watermelon.

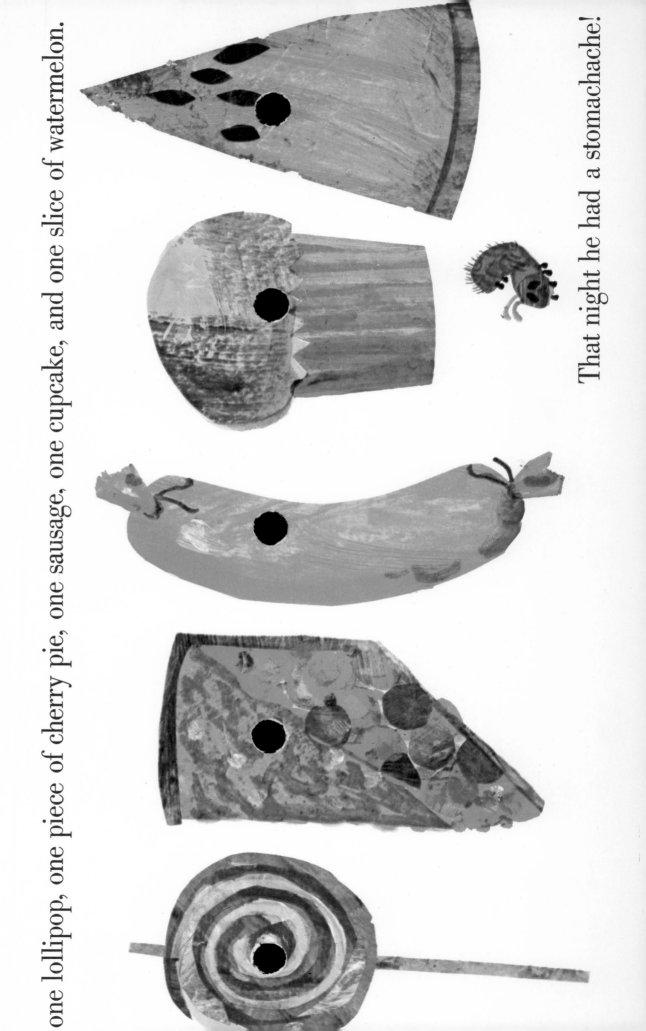

That night he had a stomachache!

The next day was Sunday again.
The caterpillar ate through
one nice green leaf,
and after that he felt
much better.

Now he wasn't hungry any more—and he wasn't a little caterpillar any more.
He was a big, fat caterpillar.

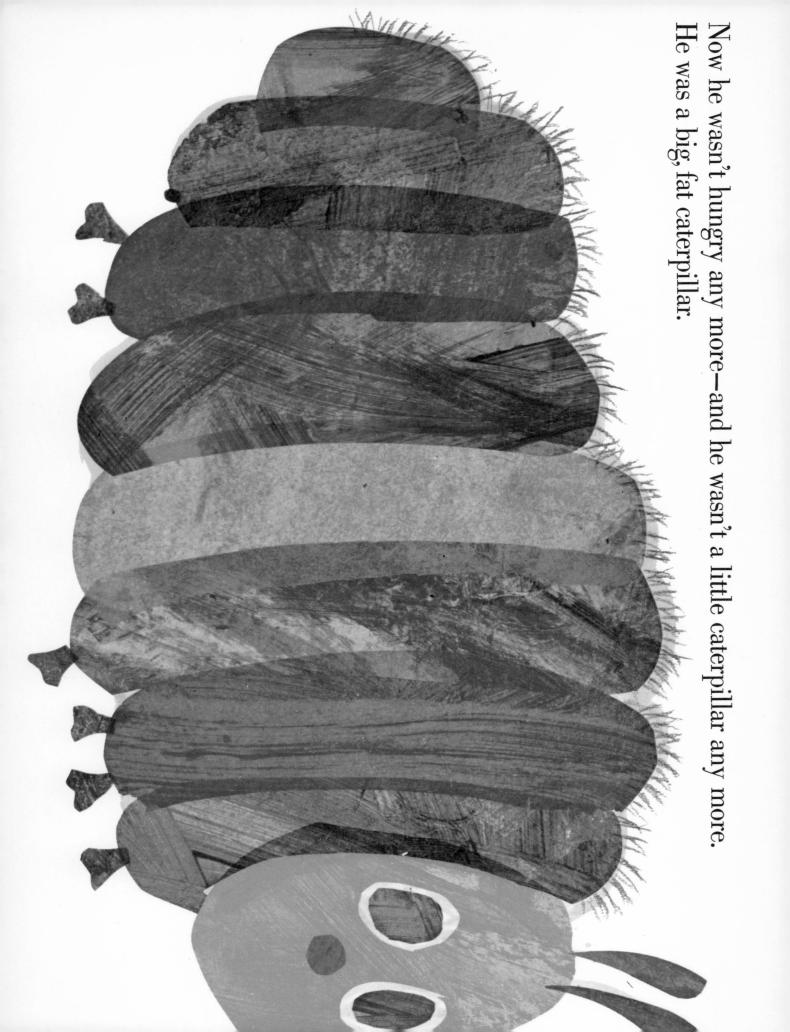

He built a small house, called a cocoon, around himself. He stayed inside for more than two weeks. Then he nibbled a hole in the cocoon, pushed his way out and . . .

he was a beautiful butterfly!

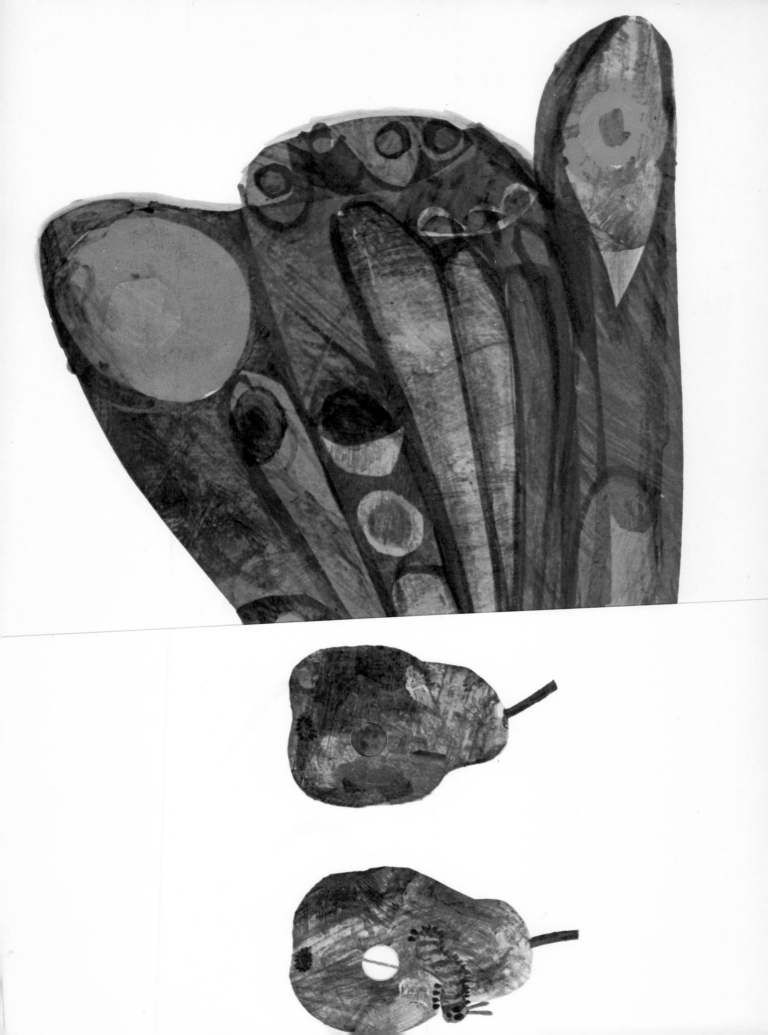